CAPTURED OFF GUARD

The Attack on Pearl Harbor

by Donald **Lemke**

illustrated by Claude **St. Aubin**

Librarian Reviewer
Laurie K. Holland
Media Specialist (National Board Certified), Edina, MN
MA in Elementary Education, Minnesota State University, Mankato

Reading Consultant
Elizabeth Stedem
Educator/Consultant, Colorado Springs, CO
MA in Elementary Education, University of Denver, CO

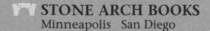 **STONE ARCH BOOKS**
Minneapolis   San Diego

Graphic Flash is published by Stone Arch Books
151 Good Counsel Drive, P.O. Box 669
Mankato, Minnesota 56002
www.stonearchbooks.com

Library of Congress Cataloging-in-Publication Data
Lemke, Donald B.
    Captured Off Guard: The Attack on Pearl Harbor / by Donald Lemke;
illustrated by Claude St. Aubin.
      p. cm. — (Graphic Flash)
      ISBN 978-1-4342-0443-1 (library binding)
      ISBN 978-1-4342-0493-6 (paperback)
      1. Graphic novels. I. St. Aubin, Claude. II. Title.
PN6727.L45C37 2008
741.5'973—dc22   2007032234

Summary: While camping out on the island of Oahu, Hawaii, Hank and his best
friend, James, hear loud explosions. Suddenly, Japanese planes fill the sky. Pearl
Harbor is under attack! James wants to hide out, but Hank wants to capture the
battle on his trusty camera. Will this budding photographer risk his life to get the
snapshot of a lifetime?

Art Director: Heather Kindseth
Graphic Designer: Brann Garvey

1 2 3 4 5 6 13 12 11 10 09 08

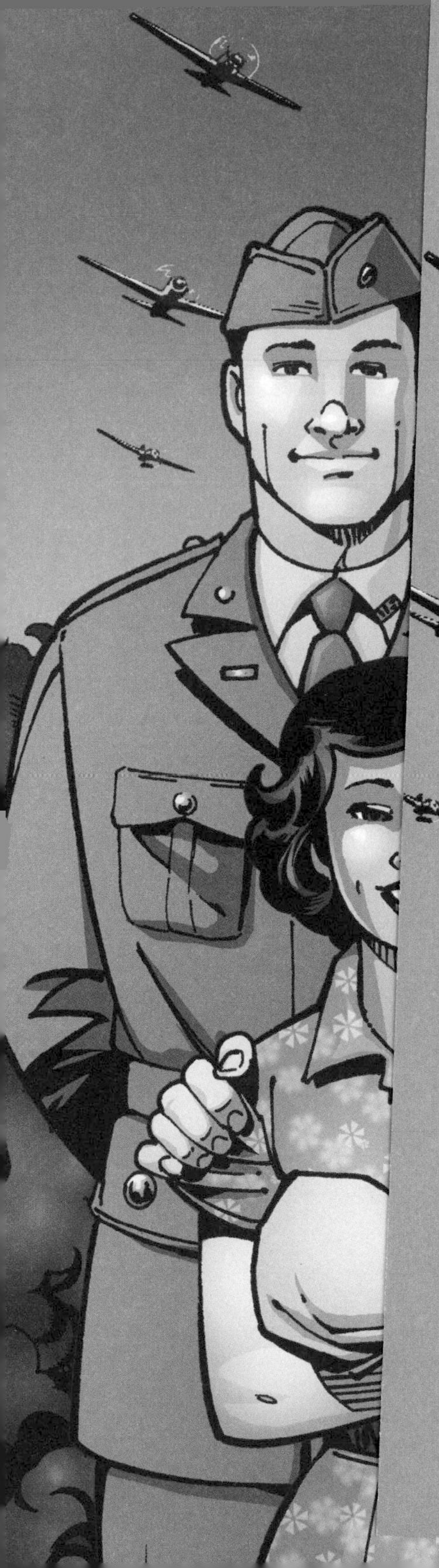

TABLE OF CONTENTS

Where is it?

I know there's an extra roll in here somewhere.

What's all the noise?

I'm trying to put your *kaikaina* down for a nap.

Chapter 1

HANK'S CAMERA

Hank looked up just long enough to see his mother in the doorway. She swayed gently from side to side trying to comfort his baby brother.

"James will be here any minute," Hank said, burying his face in the cluttered drawer.

Two o'clock. Campout at Hau Bush. Hank had stared at these words on his calendar for nearly three months. Eighty-seven days to be exact. He had marked off each day with a giant red X.

Now, December 6, 1941, had finally arrived. His best friend would soon arrive for their first overnight camping trip. Every item on Hank's detailed list was packed, except for the most important supply — his camera film.

Two years ago for his th
Hank received a small Kod
grandmother. His eye had
camera's viewfinder ever si
school, he would bike arou
other towns near his home
If he spotted a rare bird or
palm, he'd skid to a stop a

"I'm out of film," Hank
drawer and giving up his s

"Your father has plenty
mother said. "Just stop on

Hank cringed. That's ex
trying to avoid.

"You know how Papa fe
Hank said, hanging the ca

"He just wishes you wou
time at the store," she said.

The boys raced along Makule Road. Hank played catch-up as usual, trying to weave in and out of cars as quickly as his friend. He stood up, leaned forward, and pedaled harder. The leather camera strap rubbed against his sweaty neck.

He still hadn't decided whether to stop at his father's store. By the time the boys reached town, however, Hank's legs burned like lava.

"Why are you stopping? You tired already?" James yelled back at Hank.

"I have to pick up some film," he replied. "You want pictures of the fish we catch, right?"

James waited outside while Hank entered the store. At the counter, his father was hunched over a newspaper talking to Mr. Jenkins, a soldier from the nearby naval base called Pearl Harbor.

Bang! The door slammed shut behind Hank.

"Hankie Junior!" the soldier exclaimed. "Your pa was just telling me about the camping trip. I thought you'd have the tent up by now."

"I need some film," Hank said, softly.

"Ah yes, my son the photographer," Hank's father joked. He shook his head and turned to grab a roll of film off the shelf.

Hank grabbed the film and bolted out the front door. He picked up his bike, and with a running jump onto the seat, he was headed down the road.

A few moments later, James caught up with him. "Wow! I've never seen you move so fast," he said, looking surprised.

"You want to get to the beach before dark, don't you?" Hank shot back. He wasn't going to let anything ruin this trip.

When they reached Hau Bush, the boys quickly found a level spot in the sand and set up their tent. Then, James grabbed his fishing pole, and Hank grabbed his camera.

For the rest of the day, the boys enjoyed the cool winds coming off Mamala Bay. They built a fire as the sun set and feasted on the fresh fish and chunks of ripe pineapple.

Soon, only a few coals smoldered in the fire pit. James slipped off into the tent and fell asleep. Hank laid down in the sand beneath a perfectly clear sky. He watched the waves crash against the shore. Lit by the full moon, the black and white water reminded him of a photograph.

Papa doesn't understand, he thought. Hank didn't want the store. He wanted to take photos of things he'd never seen and places he'd never been before.

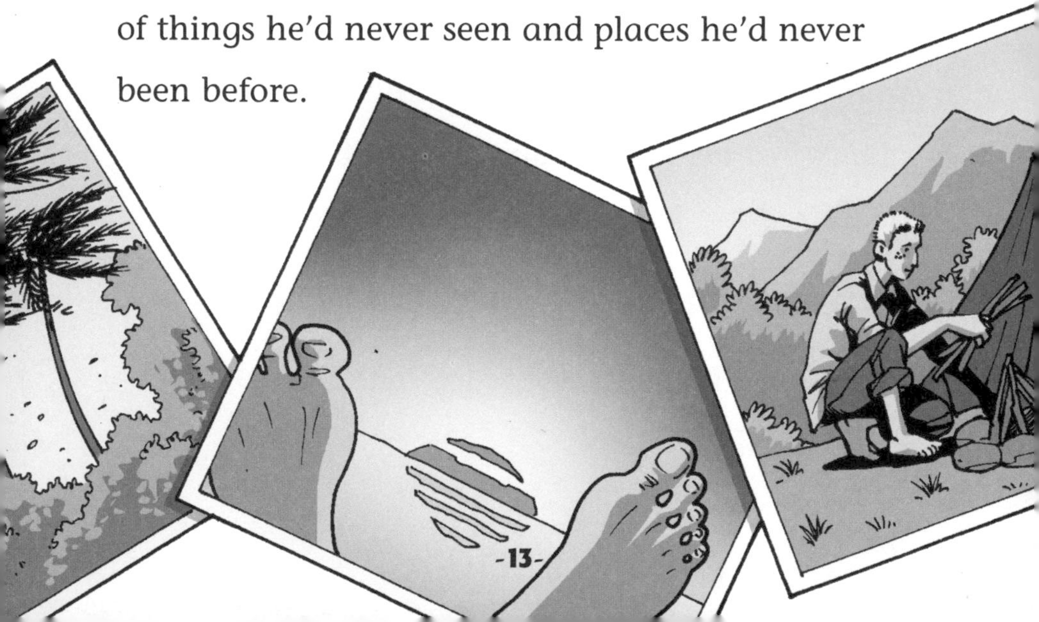

Chapter 2

THE SKY TURNED BLACK

Booooom!

A loud noise startled Hank. He sprang to his feet and looked around. The sun was up and the side of his face was covered with sticky sand.

I must have fallen asleep, he thought. Hank bent down, picked up his camera, and started brushing it clean.

Boom! Another thundering sound rolled in from the east, nearly knocking him over. Hank glanced at his watch. Almost eight o'clock. When he looked up, James was storming out of the tent.

"What's going on?" James shouted.

"Sounds like target practice," Hank replied.

They were both used to hearing the military at Pearl Harbor fire off practice rounds. But never this early, and never on Sunday.

The booming continued, and the boys decided to pack up the gear and head home. Hank started wrapping up the tent. Then suddenly, he spotted something over the hill behind them.

The boys stood in shock. They watched silently as the smoke blackened the clear, blue sky. Within moments, they could barely see the sun.

"The smoke looks like it's coming from Pearl Harbor," yelled Hank.

"Forget the tent!" shouted James. "Let's go!"

They hopped on their bikes and pedaled hard through the sand. Seconds later, they stopped.

The plane banked toward the ground, a ribbon of smoke trailing behind it like a kite's tail. Hank spotted a white star underneath its left wing.

"It's one of our guys!" he yelled. Hank had seen the silvery planes before. Dozens of them lined U.S. military airfields near his house.

Ka-boom! The plane exploded into the ground. Its flaming shell skidded across a road and plowed into a group of tall kiawe trees.

"Whoa!" Hank and James turned toward each other, stunned. As the downed plane burned, a loud whistling sound screamed behind them.

"Look, James, another one!" Hank exclaimed, pointing inland. A second silver plane roared toward them, smoke swirling out of its propeller. This one veered left, plunging into the surf, and throwing water in the air.

"What's going on?" James asked.

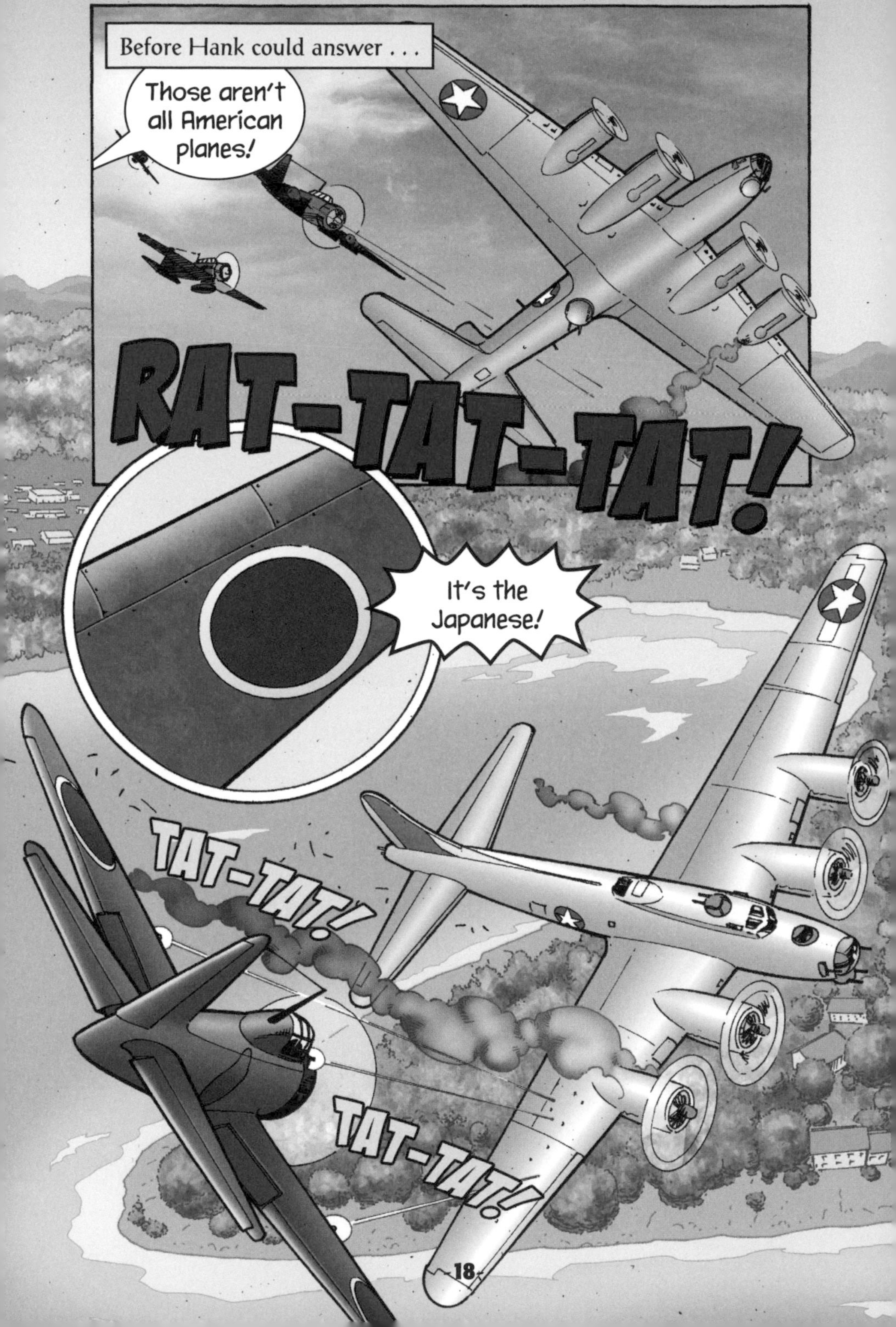
Before Hank could answer . . .
Those aren't all American planes!
RAT-TAT-TAT!
It's the Japanese!
TAT-TAT!
TAT-TAT!

Hank recognized the Japanese fighter planes from photos in magazines at his father's store. Now, one was right above him, peppering a U.S. bomber with its machine guns. Thick smoke spewed from bullet holes in the side of the bomber. The American pilot struggled to control his doomed plane. With only a moment to spare, he opened the escape hatch and jumped out.

The boys watched the empty bomber slam onto the beach and burst into a giant fireball. A second later, the pilot's parachute opened, and he drifted into a group of trees.

"Come on," James yelled, spinning his bike around in the sand. "He might need our help!"

Hank followed his friend. Looking up at the sky, he saw the Japanese fighter planes turn and head back toward Pearl Harbor. Hank didn't know what was going on, but he knew something was seriously wrong.

The boys ducked into a gas station. Dozens of local residents were huddled inside. In the corner, a woman covered her baby's ears against the explosions. At the back door, a man tore a piece of cloth to bandage his wounded hand. Others crowded around a radio at the front counter.

"Are you boys okay?" a man at the counter asked them.

"His leg is bleeding, but I think we're all right," Hank replied, trying to catch his breath. "What's happening out there?"

"That's what we're trying to find out," the man said, putting his ear to the radio and jiggling the knobs.

Hank and James moved in closer, waiting to hear something, anything, about the situation. After a few moments, a loud man's voice barked through the static.

The radio announcer repeated the words over and over. Hank and James looked at each other, wondering what to do. Then, the man standing near the back door spoke up.

"I'm heading to the sugar cane fields," he said. "Who's coming with me?"

The group stood silently, waiting for someone to answer. Hank looked toward the front window. Sirens started to blare and dozens of military trucks rolled through the town.

"The man on the radio said to stay put," the woman with the baby said.

"Every building in this town is a target," the man said, raising his voice. "The sugar cane fields are the safest place until the attack is over."

Some of the other residents agreed and started heading for the door. James pulled Hank aside.

"What are we going to do, Hank?" he asked. "I think we should hide in the fields."

For the first time since that morning, Hank felt the weight of the camera around his neck. He looked back up at the window. Through the glass, the action seemed to stop, like the moment before a photograph. Hank knew what he had to do.

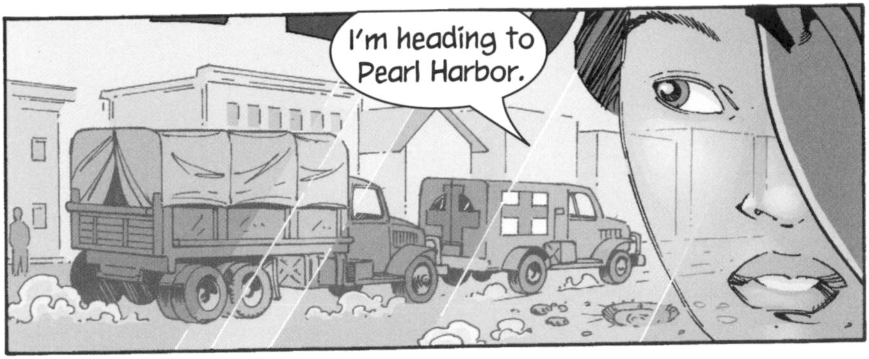
I'm heading to Pearl Harbor.

"Are you crazy?" James yelled, grabbing Hank. "It's not safe. Besides, I can't make it that far."

Hank looked down at James's right leg. His jeans were stained red with blood from the knee down. "I know," Hank said, "I'm going alone."

He didn't have time to explain. Hank hugged his friend, clutched his camera tight, and then headed out the door.

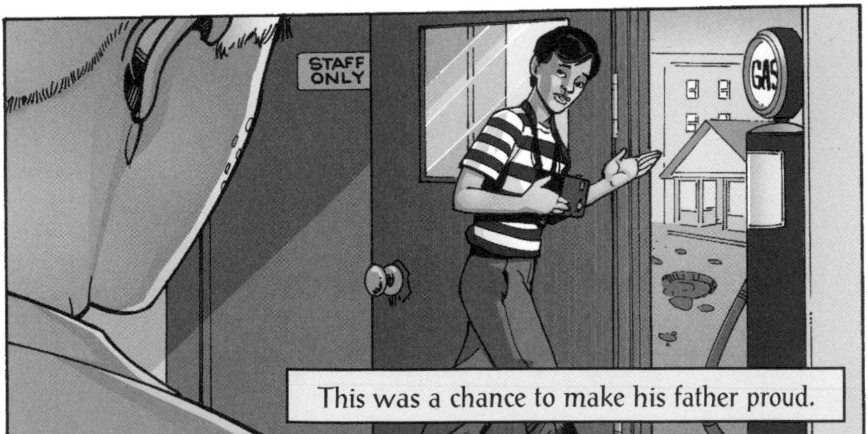
STAFF ONLY
GAS
This was a chance to make his father proud.

Chapter 3
UNDER ATTACK!

Outside, swarms of Japanese fighter planes were buzzing overhead. Hank sprinted down the road, which was pitted with craters and littered with old cars. He searched for his bike. Nothing. *Maybe this was a bad idea,* Hank thought.

He looked back at the gas station. James and the others were leaving, headed in the direction of the sugar cane fields. If he ran fast enough, he could still follow them to safety. Military trucks and ambulances rushed past in the other direction, toward Pearl Harbor.

"No!" Hank yelled, out loud. "I'm not going to sit around and hide." He started walking, following the dusty trail of military vehicles.

The sky had turned nearly as black as night and flames burst all around him. The road wasn't safe, so he scrambled into the woods. Branches and leaves slashed at his face and hands.

But he kept running . . .

He reached higher ground and a better view of the harbor.

Oh no!

On the hill, Hank looked down at Pearl Harbor. For a moment, he couldn't move. He stood completely frozen with shock.

Hank had often biked past the harbor. Each time, he would stop and snap pictures of the eight giant ships docked along Battleship Row. Their large, silver hulls cast perfect reflections onto the turquoise water.

Hank had memorized each one of their names, labeling every photo he developed. Now, half of the battleships were on fire, throwing thick smoke from the top of their masts. The water had turned into an inky pool of oil. Thousands of U.S. soldiers darted in every direction. The whole scene was too much for Hank. Without thinking, he picked up his camera and put his eye on the viewfinder.

Through the camera's lens, Hank scanned the harbor, trying to focus on a single image.

Then, Hank saw what looked like a group of planes approaching on the horizon. He snapped a picture. For a brief moment, the camera's shutter closed and the viewfinder went black. When it opened, Hank could clearly see the markings on the planes.

A second attack wave! The Japanese fighters and bombers dove into the harbor like a group of hungry birds. Immediately, sailors on the USS *Tennessee,* USS *Maryland,* and other battleships began firing their anti-aircraft guns. Black puffs of smoke burst in the sky, hitting several Japanese planes, which spiraled into the harbor.

The battleships continued taking heavy fire. The USS *Pennsylvania,* docked at the navy yard, exploded in a flurry of bomber attacks. Smaller destroyers and cruiser ships started to sink beneath the oily water. Still, nothing could have prepared Hank for what he saw next.

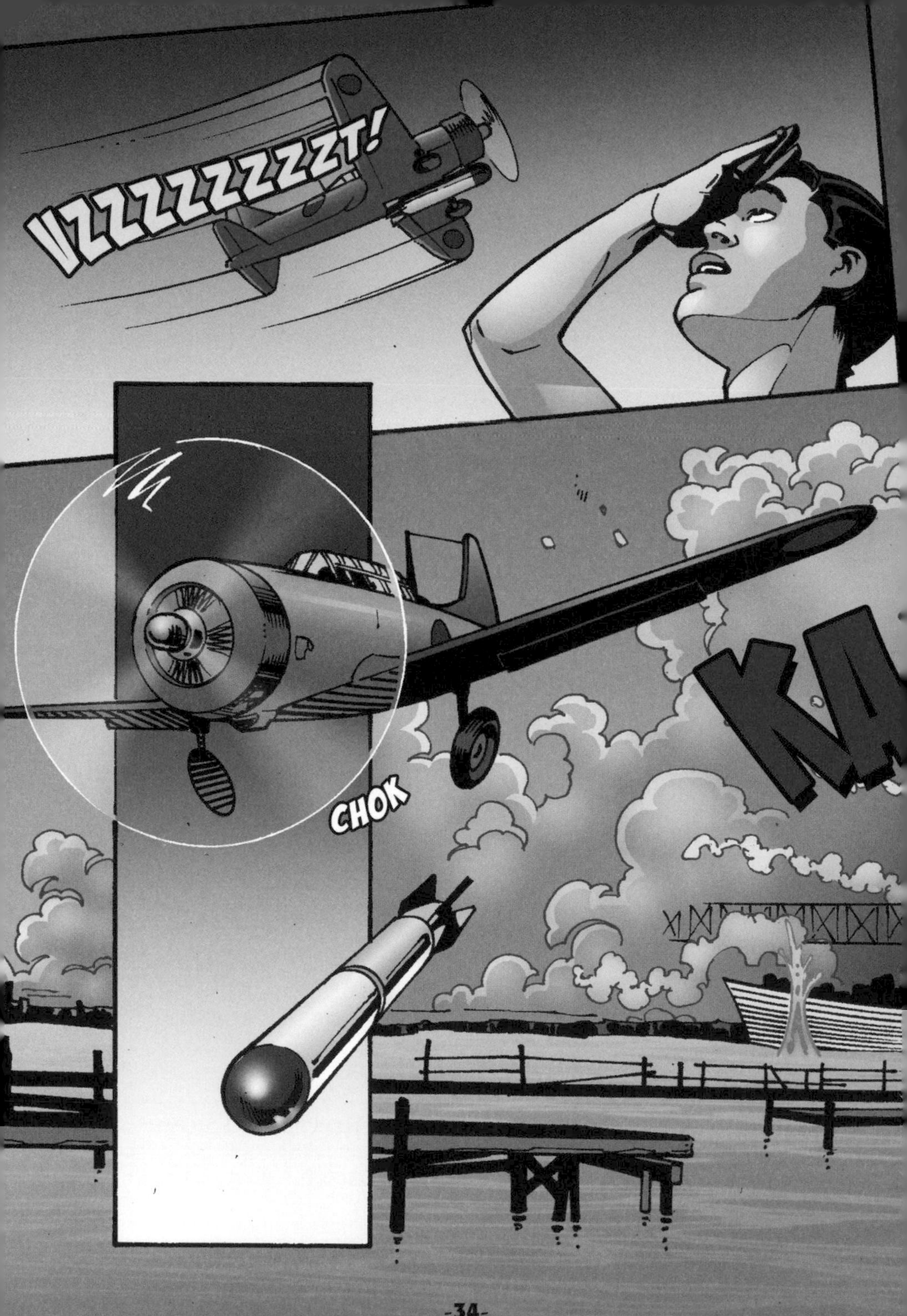
VZZZZZZZZZT!
CHOK
KA

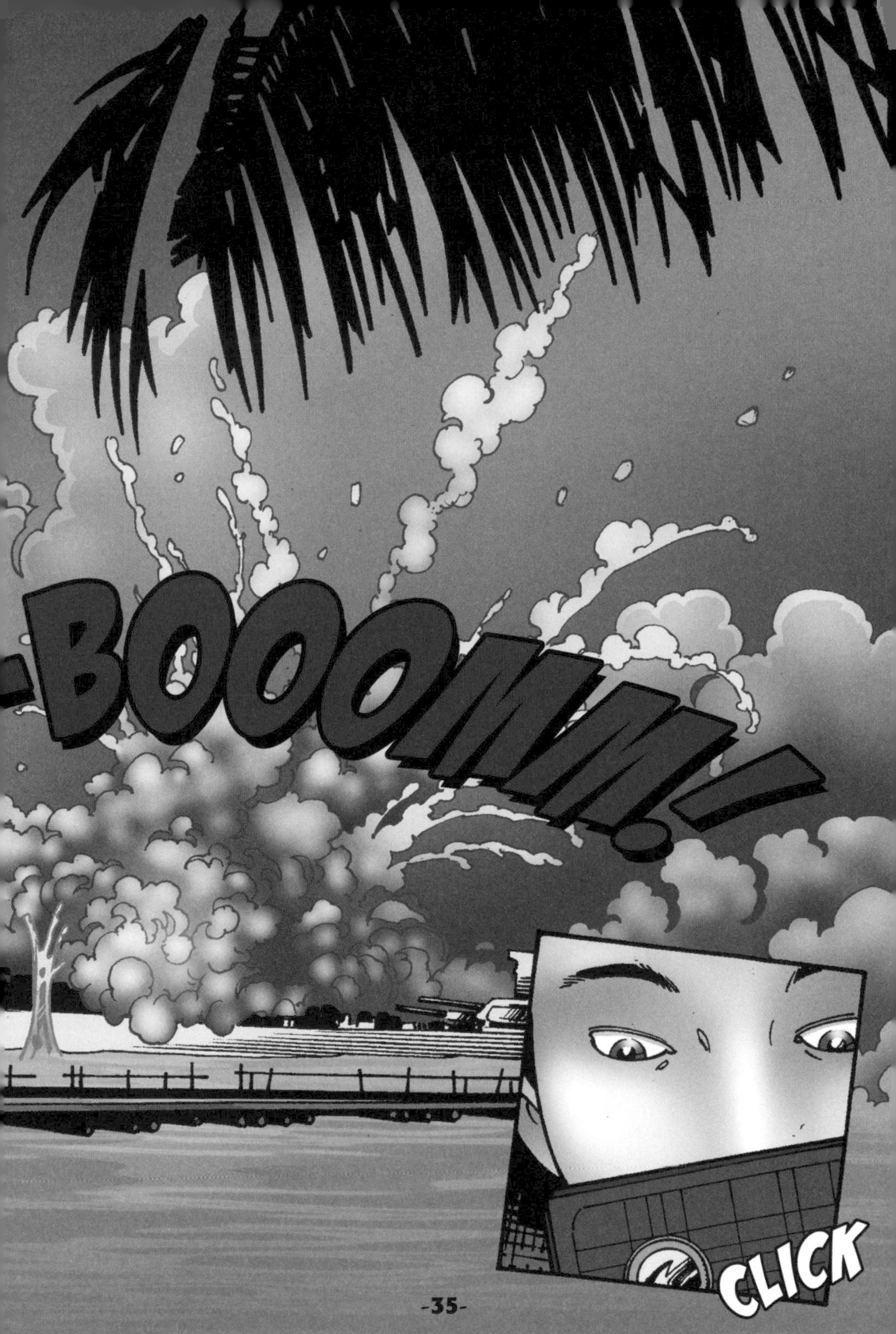

BOOOMM!!
CLICK

Hank felt the heat of the explosion against his face. He tried to snap another picture, but the film was gone! He took off the camera from around his neck and placed it on the ground. Then, he searched frantically through his pockets for another roll of film.

Suddenly, a voice shouted up from the road below, "Hank, is that you?"

Who knows I'm up here? Hank wondered. He started down toward the road, peering through the trees and trying to get a better look.

"Mr. Jenkins!" Hank yelled. He saw his father's friend waving from inside an old military truck. Hank scurried down the hill.

"What are you doing?" asked Mr. Jenkins. "It's not safe out here."

Hank looked down at the ground, trying to think of an excuse. "I, uh, I was just —"

"It doesn't matter," Mr. Jenkin's interrupted. "I just learned the 'Ewa airfield has been attacked!"

"Mama!" Hank exclaimed. The airfield was close to his house. "Mr. Jenkins, is my family all right?"

Chapter 4

FINDING HIS FAMILY

The old truck rattled toward 'Ewa Beach. In the distance, Hank spotted dark smoke rising from the airfield. He felt ashamed. How could he have left his family alone for so long? His mother would be worried sick, if she was still okay.

When they finally reached the town, Mr. Jenkins slowed the truck to a crawl. Hank looked around, scanning the area for a familiar face. Most of the residents had retreated to their homes and the road was nearly empty. Several cars had their tires blown out and were splattered with bullet holes.

Mr. Jenkins turned the corner onto Hank's street. "Stop, Mr. Jenkins!" Hank yelled. "Stop!"

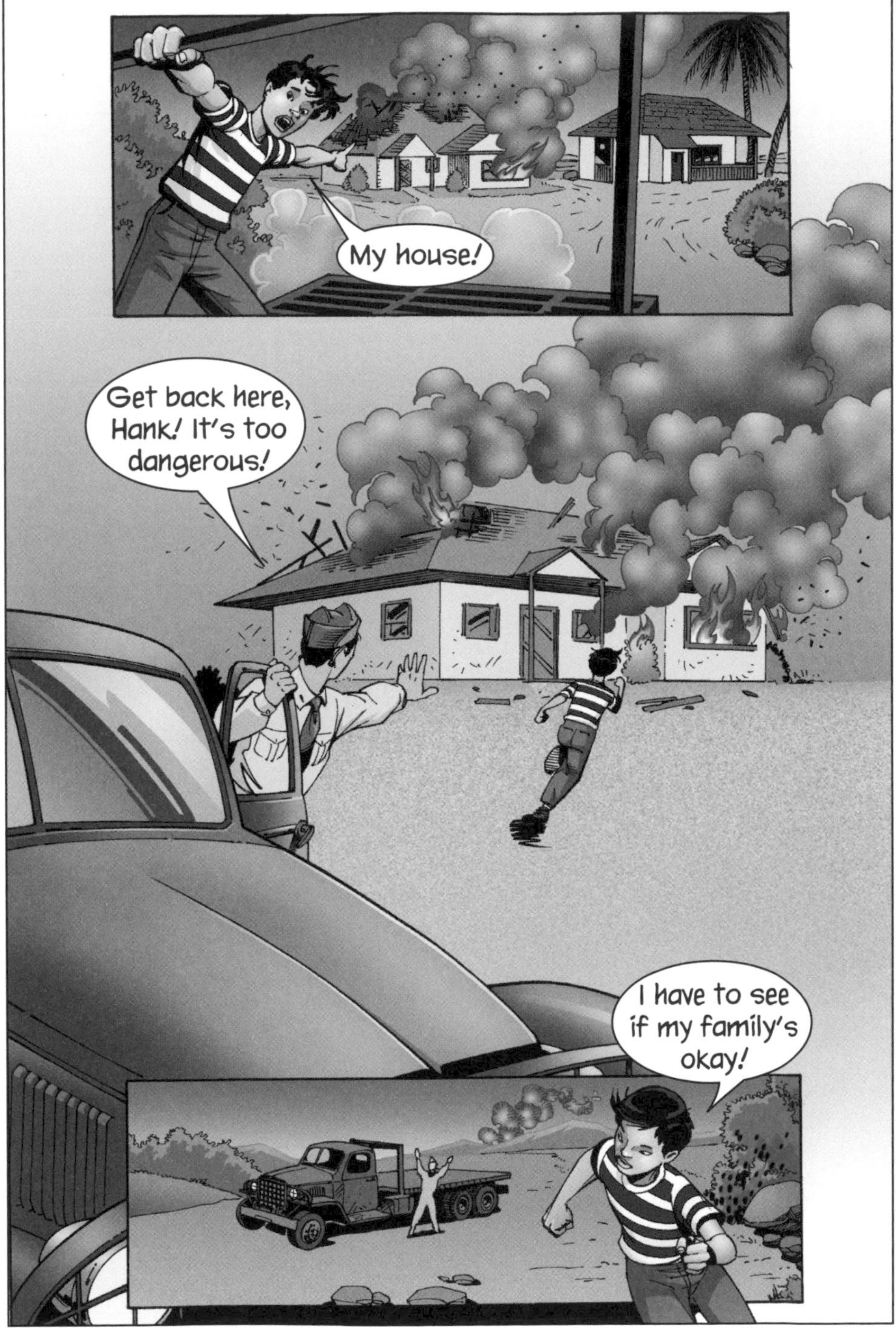
My house!
Get back here, Hank! It's too dangerous!
I have to see if my family's okay!

Hank ran into the house. Inside, the walls of the living room dripped with flames. He yelled for his mother. No answer. Hank hurried down the hallway, stepping over shattered floorboards and dodging falling embers. When he finally reached his room, Hank pounded open the door with his shoulder.

Peaceful pictures that once plastered Hank's walls now covered his floor. Hank bent down. He spotted his favorite one of them all.

It was taken two months ago, a week after his baby brother was born. James had been there, too, but he offered to take the photograph. This was the only picture Hank had of his whole family together. Now, he worried that his chances of seeing them all again were slipping away.

"Mama!" Hank shouted, slumping to the floor.

"Hank?" a muffled voice cried out from the hallway.

Hank rushed out of the bedroom. The hallway was turning into a smoke-filled chimney. He fell to his knees and started crawling along the floor.

"Mama, where are you?" he yelled.

"In here, Hank! We're trapped!" Hank heard pounding from inside the hall closet. When he got closer, Hank saw his mother's delicate fingers reaching out through a crack in the doorway. The door was blocked! As the hallway filled with smoke, Hank scrambled to remove the boards.

Hank and his mother slid off the front porch, coughing and wheezing. Once he caught his breath, Hank hugged his mother and kissed his baby brother on the forehead. It had been less than a day since he last saw them, but it felt like everything had changed.

"Where's Papa?" Hank asked.

"He never came home from the store," his mother replied, sounding worried.

Hank looked back at the road. Mr. Jenkins was still there, waving the family into his truck. They hopped in and took off toward the store. On the way, Hank heard more planes roar in the sky.

Hank didn't see any more Japanese planes as the truck sped down the road. By the time they reached the store, he wondered if the fighting had finally ended.

Hank helped his mother into the store. Inside, dozens of local residents greeted them. Their neighbor Ms. Wong, Hank's teacher Mr. Miller, even his little league coach, were all there. They had come for shelter and to wait out the attack.

Hank spotted his father. He was near the counter, handing out food and supplies.

"I tried to make it home, but the roads were blocked," his father said, nearly crying. "Then people started showing up for help."

"It's okay, Papa," Hank said. "We're all okay."

He hugged his father and thought about the morning. Hank couldn't wait to show him the photographs he had taken. He could prove that he hadn't been afraid. He hadn't just sat around.

Hank pulled away from his father and looked down for his camera.

Hank's camera was gone! He grabbed at his neck. *It couldn't have fallen off,* he thought. *I would have heard it drop!*

"What's wrong, Hank?" his father asked.

"I lost my camera!" Hank gasped, frantically looking around the room.

"It's okay, son," his father said. "I can order you a new one."

"You don't understand," Hank sobbed. "All of my pictures. Everything that happened this morning. I wanted to show you —"

His father headed back to the front counter. Hank watched as he continued handing out supplies to anyone in need. Until that moment, Hank hadn't realized how important the store and his father were to this town.

Bang! A loud noise startled Hank, and he spun around expecting the worst this time.

James's leg was bandaged at the knee, and he was limping. Hank walked toward him.

"What took you so long," Hank joked, not knowing what to say.

James looked down at his injured leg. "Very, funny," he said. James knew his friend was glad to see him.

During the next few days, Hank thought about searching for his camera, but he helped his father at the store instead. He stocked shelves, wiped down the counters, and swept broken glass off the front porch.

While there, Hank and his father listened to the president on the radio talk about the attack. In the newspapers, they read about the thousands of soldiers that died at Pearl Harbor. They read that the United States had declared war on Japan.

"I'm too old," Hank's father said, reading the paper. "But I wish I could help out the country."

"You already do, Papa," Hank said, looking at the long line of customers.

In the coming months, U.S. soldiers fought battles half a world away, and Hank continued working for his father. Then one day, a package arrived at the store.

"Thanks, Papa!" Hank exclaimed.

Hank's father continued sweeping the floor.

"I know you'll put it to good use," he said, not looking up.

Hank thought about his missing camera. It had been filled with dozens of photographs he would never see again. But now, Hank knew, he'd have the chance to take many more.

United States Navy

November 10, 1943

Dear Mama and Papa,

I just arrived in Mar

thought you'd want to

me in my new uniform.

ABOUT THE AUTHOR

Growing up in a small Minnesota town, Donald Lemke kept himself busy reading anything from comic books to classic novels. Today, Lemke works as a children's book editor and pursues a master's degree in publishing from Hamline University in St. Paul, Minnesota. Lemke has written a variety of children's books and graphic novels. His ideas often come to him while running along the inspiring trails near his home.

ABOUT THE ILLUSTRATOR

Claude St. Aubin was born in Ontario, Canada. He went to college in Montreal, Quebec, where he graduated with a degree in graphic design. After working for a Canadian comic book publisher for a short time, St. Aubin pursued a career as a graphic designer. Soon, however, he returned to his true passion as a comic book artist. St. Aubin is happily married with two children.

GLOSSARY

airfield (AIR-feeld)—an area where airplanes take off and land

aloha (uh-LOH-hah)—a word meaning both hello or good-bye in the Hawaiian language

anti-aircraft guns (AN-tee-air-kraft GUNZ)— weapons fired from the ground at planes overhead

battleship (BAT-uhl-ship)—a heavily armed ship made for war

'Ewa Beach (EE-vah BEECH)—a district in the city of Honolulu, which is located on the island of Oahu, Hawaii

kaikaina (kah-ee-kah-EE-nah)—in the Hawaiian language, a younger sibling of the same gender

kiawe (KEE-ah-vay)—a tree common on the Hawaiian Islands

McCoy (mih-KOI)—something that is not fake; the phrase "the real McCoy" means "the real thing."

veered (VEERD)—to turn suddenly

viewfinder (VYOO-fyn-duhr)—the part of a camera through which a person looks

MORE ABOUT PEARL HARBOR

The attack on Pearl Harbor ended just before 10:00 in the morning on December 7, 1941. In less than two hours of fighting, 2,403 Americans died and more than 1,100 people were wounded.

The U.S. Pacific Fleet was heavily damaged in the attack. The Japanese planes sank or damaged 21 American ships including eight battleships, USS *Arizona*, USS *California*, USS *Maryland*, USS *Nevada*, USS *Oklahoma*, USS *Pennsylvania*, USS *Tennessee*, and USS *West Virginia*. The United States also lost 188 aircraft.

The first wave of Japanese dive bombers and fighters to hit Pearl Harbor included 181 planes. The second wave of the attack added 170 more. Of these 351 planes, only 29 of them were lost.

One day after the attack, December 8, 1941, President Franklin D. Roosevelt asked the U.S. Congress to declare war on Japan. Soon after, American troops would become an important part of World War II (1939–1945).

In 1962, a national memorial to the victims of the Pearl Harbor attack opened in Honolulu, Hawaii. The memorial rests atop the waters of the harbor, directly above the sunken USS *Arizona*.

Truth Behind the Story

Even today, the photographers behind the most famous Pearl Harbor photos remain unknown. One legend says that these pictures were found in an old Brownie camera, which had been stored in a locker for many years. Most people believe the story can't be true and the pictures were probably taken by official U.S. Navy photographers. Still, it's fun to imagine that a young photographer like Hank could have played a part in history.

DISCUSSION QUESTIONS

1. On page 27, Hank decides to head to Pearl Harbor instead of hiding in the sugar cane fields. Do you think this was a good decision? Why or why not? Why do you believe he made this choice?

2. Near the end of the story, Hank's camera is suddenly gone. Where do you think he lost it? Look for clues in the text and illustrations that support your answer.

3. Hank thought that his father didn't like his photography hobby. Then why do you think he bought Hank a new camera?

WRITING PROMPTS

1. This story is known as historical fiction. The historical event, in this case Pearl Harbor, is true, but the characters are fiction. Choose your favorite historical event. Then make up a story that happens on that day.

2. Hank's favorite hobby was taking photographs. Describe your favorite hobby and why you like the activity so much.

3. At the end of the story, Hank becomes a Navy photographer. Imagine you are the author. Describe what happens to some of the other characters in the book, such as James, Mama, or Mr. Jenkins.

INTERNET SITES

Do you want to know more about subjects related to this book? Or are you interested in learning about other topics? Then check out FactHound, a fun, easy way to find Internet sites.

Our investigative staff has already sniffed out great sites for you!

Here's how to use FactHound:

1. Visit *www.facthound.com*

2. Select your grade level.

3. To learn more about subjects related to this book, type in the book's ISBN number: **9781434204431**.

4. Click the **Fetch It** button.

FactHound will fetch the best Internet sites for you.

AR
BL-43
Pts- 1.0
Quiz#- 119921